BOB BOOKS.

The New Puppy

by LYNN MASLEN KERTELL
illustrated by SUE HENDRA

SCHOLASTIC INC.

ISBN 978-1-338-80512-3

10 9 8 7 6 5 4 3 2 1   22 23 24 25 26

Printed in the U.S.A.   40
This edition first printing 2022

Jack and Anna want a puppy.

A puppy is a friend.

A puppy likes to play.

"A puppy is a lot of work,"
say Mom and Dad.

"Puppies need to be fed," says Dad.

"Puppies need to go out," says Mom.

"We will take care of it,"
the kids say.

10

Jack and Anna can do a
good job.

There are many dogs at the
pet shelter.

Big dogs, small dogs,
fluffy dogs, shaggy dogs.

Jack and Anna like
the brown puppy.

The puppy gives Anna a kiss.

"What will you name your pet?"
asks Mom.

"We can call him Buddy!"
says Jack.

Buddy loves to chase a ball.

He loves to tug a rope.

Jack and Anna want to draw.

Buddy wants to help.

Jack and Anna make a fort.

Buddy jumps in.

"Time to go out," says Mom.

Buddy runs and runs.

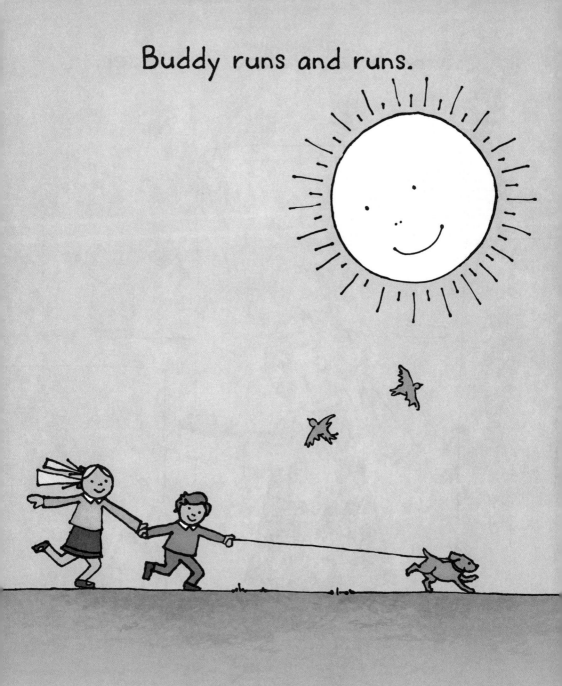

Anna gives Buddy his dinner.

Jack gives him water.

Buddy is tired.

Buddy falls fast asleep.

29

Tomorrow, Buddy will be ready
to play again.

BOB BOOKS.

The Complete Bob Books® Series

READING READINESS

MY FIRST BOB BOOKS ® PRE-READING SKILLS

MY FIRST BOB BOOKS ® ALPHABET

STAGE 1: STARTING TO READ

SET 1 BEGINNING READERS

MORE BEGINNING READERS

FIRST STORIES

RHYMING WORDS

STAGE 2: EMERGING READER

ADVANCING BEGINNERS

SIGHT WORDS KINDERGARTEN

ANIMAL STORIES

SIGHT WORDS FIRST GRADE

STAGE 3: DEVELOPING READER

WORD FAMILIES

COMPLEX WORDS

LONG VOWELS

SCHOLASTIC